play forever on video and **Disney DVD**

Published by Ladybird Books Ltd.
A Penguin Company
Penguin Books Ltd., 80 Strand, London WC2R 0RL
Penguin Books Australia Ltd., Camberwell, Victoria, Australia
Penguin Books (NZ) Ltd., Private Bag 102902, NSMC, Auckland,
New Zealand
Copyright © 2004 Disney Enterprises, Inc.
All rights reserved.
LADYBIRD and the device of a ladybird
are trademarks of Ladybird Books, Ltd.
4 6 8 10 9 7 5
Printed in Italy

WALT DISNEY'S

CLASSIC

TARZAN

Ladybird

Deep in the jungle, a baby was crying. Not long ago, he and his parents had survived a shipwreck. They then lived safely in a tree house – until Sabor the leopard found them.

When Sabor strode away from the house, only the baby was left alive.

A gorilla named Kala heard the baby crying. A few days ago, Kala's own baby had been taken by Sabor, and she was still sad. Now another baby was in trouble. So Kala followed the sound.

Kala gently lifted the human baby from its cradle, and the little boy stopped crying. Kala felt her heart leap with love.

Kala named the baby Tarzan, and he grew into a happy, lively little boy. He loved hanging from vines and scaring his mother.

Tarzan made many friends in the jungle, but his favourite was a young gorilla named Terk. One day, Terk dared Tarzan to go and get an elephant hair and Tarzan said he'd do it.

Tarzan didn't mean to startle the elephants, but he did and they stampeded. The other gorillas were almost trampled by the terrified herd.

When Kerchak, the gorillas' leader, found out what had happened, he was furious. "Someone could have been killed because of you!" he told Tarzan.

"He's only a child," said Kala. "He'll learn."

"He will never learn!" shouted Kerchak. "He will never be one of us!"

Later, Kala found Tarzan smearing mud
on his face. He was trying to make
himself look more like an ape.

"Why am I so different?" he asked.

In reply, Kala put Tarzan's hand on his
chest, so he could feel his heart beating.
Then she pressed his ear to *her* heart.

"See?" she said. "Our heartbeats are
exactly the same."

Tarzan understood. As he hugged Kala,
he decided he would try to make Kerchak
proud of him, too.

Years passed, and Tarzan grew strong. He learnt to survive in the jungle.

One day, Terk and Tarzan were wrestling playfully near the gorillas' nest, when suddenly, Sabor leapt out.

Kerchak grabbed the leopard. As they struggled, Sabor wounded Kerchak with her razor-sharp claws, then moved in for the kill.

Swinging from a vine, Tarzan kicked Sabor and threw her off balance. Tarzan lured Sabor away from the wounded Kerchak, into some bushes. The gorillas held their breath until Tarzan emerged, holding Sabor's body above him.

A moment later, a loud bang sent
everyone rushing for cover. But Tarzan
was curious and went to investigate.

Hiding in the bushes, Tarzan saw three
strange creatures approaching. They were
humans – and one was carrying a rifle.

One of the humans, a young woman,
began to draw a baby baboon. But the
little baboon became upset, and all the
other baboons attacked the woman.
Tarzan came to her rescue.

When the baboons had gone, Tarzan took the woman's hand and held it against his. They were alike! He gazed into her eyes. Could it be – was she a creature like him?

"Tar-zan," he said, pointing to himself.

"Jane," she said, pointing to herself.

Jane and her father, Professor Porter, had come from England to study gorillas. Their guide, a hunter called Clayton, was the one who had fired the rifle shot. Jane eagerly told them both about Tarzan, the amazing "ape man" who had saved her from the baboons.

Meanwhile, Tarzan had rejoined his family. Kerchak ordered everyone to stay away from the strangers.

"They mean us no harm," Tarzan protested.

"I don't know that," Kerchak replied. "Protect your family and stay away from them," he told Tarzan.

"Why didn't you tell me there were creatures like me?" Tarzan asked Kala.

The next day, Tarzan found his way to the humans' camp. Jane happily showed him pictures of the outside world and began teaching him English. Tarzan learned quickly.

Tarzan showed Jane his world, too – the leafy jungle plants, and the beautiful, brightly coloured birds. Professor Porter could see that a special friendship was forming between Tarzan and his daughter.

The professor himself was eager to learn all he could from Tarzan, but Clayton only wanted Tarzan to lead them to the gorillas.

At first, Tarzan refused. He knew Kerchak would be angry.

All too soon, Jane told Tarzan that she and her father were preparing to go home. "Please come with us," she said.

"Jane must stay with Tarzan," he told her. Fighting back tears, Jane said that she couldn't.

"Only one thing will keep her here," Clayton told Tarzan. "If she could see the gorillas…"

Desperate not to lose Jane, Tarzan led the humans to the gorillas. The Porters were enchanted. As Jane played with some babies, Clayton made a map showing the gorillas' location.

When Kerchak saw the humans, he charged towards Clayton.

"Go!" Tarzan shouted to the humans, as he held Kerchak back.

When the humans had gone, Kerchak glared at Tarzan. "I – I'm sorry," said Tarzan.

Kala knew it was time to show Tarzan the tree house. "I should have done this long ago," she said. There he found a picture of himself as a baby with his human parents.

"Now you know, Tarzan," said Kala, and she left him alone.

Moments later Tarzan appeared, dressed in his father's clothes. He had decided to go with the Porters and live in the human world.

"No matter where I go, you will always be my mother," he told Kala.

"And you will always be in my heart," Kala said tenderly.

The following morning, Terk and her friend Tantor watched sadly from the edge of the jungle as Tarzan, Clayton and the Porters rowed out to their ship.

Tarzan followed the Porters aboard, only to find that the deck was filled with cages. At Clayton's orders, some rough-looking men grabbed the three of them and began forcing them below deck.

"Clayton!" cried Tarzan. "Help!"

"These cages are for your furry friends," he sneered. "I'm going to sell them for three hundred pounds each. And I couldn't have done it without you! Lock them all up," he told his men.

Realising what he had done, Tarzan let out a cry of despair. Terk and Tantor heard it, and headed straight for the ship.

Meanwhile, Clayton and his men made their way to the gorillas' home, and started to capture the apes.

Suddenly Tarzan's yell pierced the air. He arrived with an army of animals, including Tantor carrying Terk and the Porters on his back. They quickly freed the gorillas.

Angrily, Clayton fired at Tarzan, wounding him. As Clayton raised his rifle again, Kerchak charged – and took the bullet meant for Tarzan.

Clayton chased Tarzan up into the trees. Tarzan grabbed Clayton's rifle and broke it against a branch. Clayton hit out wildly with his knife, but he fell from the tree. He would never trouble the gorillas again.

Tarzan ran to Kerchak.

"Forgive me," Tarzan begged.

"No!" gasped Kerchak. "You forgive me… for not understanding that you have always been one of us. Take care of our family… my son."

The next morning, Tarzan and Jane stood on the beach, saying goodbye.

"I will miss you, Jane," said Tarzan softly. He took her hand and held it against his, just as he had done when they first met.

Weeping, Jane broke away and ran to the boat where her father was waiting.

"You should stay, dear," said Professor Porter to Jane. "You love him."

Jane knew that her father was right. She jumped out of the boat and ran into Tarzan's arms. All the gorillas cheered and welcomed Jane's return. Then Professor Porter decided to stay, too.

Tarzan was with the family he loved, in his jungle home. Now, with Jane by his side, he knew that he would always be where he belonged.

Yours
to own
on ![Disney]
DVD

WALT DISNEY
CLASSICS

Magical stories to